The BEST BOOK EVER

written by **Amy Logan**

illustrated by **Rich Green**

Published by
Full Heart Publishing, Full Heart LLC
FullHeartPublishing.com
Printed in USA

First Edition, First Print
ISBN-13: 9781724940438

Get additional books at:

AuthorAmyLogan.com

To my kids, Sadie and Scott.

Every time you look in the mirror, even with crazy hair or goofy skin, may you always see yourselves the way I see you -- perfectly imperfect and beautiful and amazing and just what the world needed to make it a better place.

Love you.

Pump-pump.

Mom

Pssssssst...

Hey cool kid!

YES!

I'm talking to you.

Do you know what I'm thinking?
Should I tell it to you?

Nah,
I think I'll wait.

Although,
do you want to know
something great?

Something SUPER
and AWESOME
and GREAT times 28 ?

Hmmmm,

Maybe I should keep it
a secret for now.
If I tell you, the book
will be over and HOW
can we do that?
It's only the
start of the book!

But I'm so EXCITED to tell you!

WAIT!!!

Don't look!

(OK, you can take a small peek.)

BUT GO SLOW !!!

I'm so excited!

EEEEK!!!

WAIT!

I can't do it.
I just can't go through it.
So, I've changed my mind!

THIS is the ending.

I'm just kidding!
I'm only pretending!

But for real this time...

Are you ready for some serious news?

About what I know? I'll give you some clues...

It's about someone...

so awesome

and super

and **SWeet!**

And it's someone I think that you'd love to meet!

WAIT A MINUTE!!
you KNOW this person!!!
you know them so well!
And you already like them,
it's easy to tell.

Do you know who it is?
WHO?
who?
who?
Who?

22

TURN THE PAGE

IT'S YOU!!!

You are AWESOME,
the most
AWESOME PERSON YET!

You're AWESOMER
than awesome!
You didn't know that I'll bet!

It makes me so giddy because I think you're so cool.

well you are! HOLY COW!
It's so super true
that you are AMAZING
because YOU were born YOU!

Take a look in the mirror
and you'll see it, too.
And while you are looking,
say this to you:

Insert Photo Here

"Hey you!
You are AWESOME and FUNNY and LOVING and GREAT!
And you are so SUPER GREAT times 128!
And I LOVE YOU!
You're AMAZING, the things that you do!
You're KIND and GIVING and you're HAPPY too!
There's nothing in this world that you cannot do!"

So... what do you think?

Did you know it was

Y ou ?

I'll bet that you did.

How could you not since you're one awesome kid?

You are awesome right now and
you'll be awesome forever...

Didn't I tell you this is

the BEST BOOK EVER

Made in the USA
Lexington, KY
09 November 2019